VENEFICIA PUBLICATIONS UK
veneficiapublications.com
Typesetting © Veneficia Publications
October 2020

The Chesil Apothecary

A Magical Tale

Written & Illustrated
By

Kathy Sharp

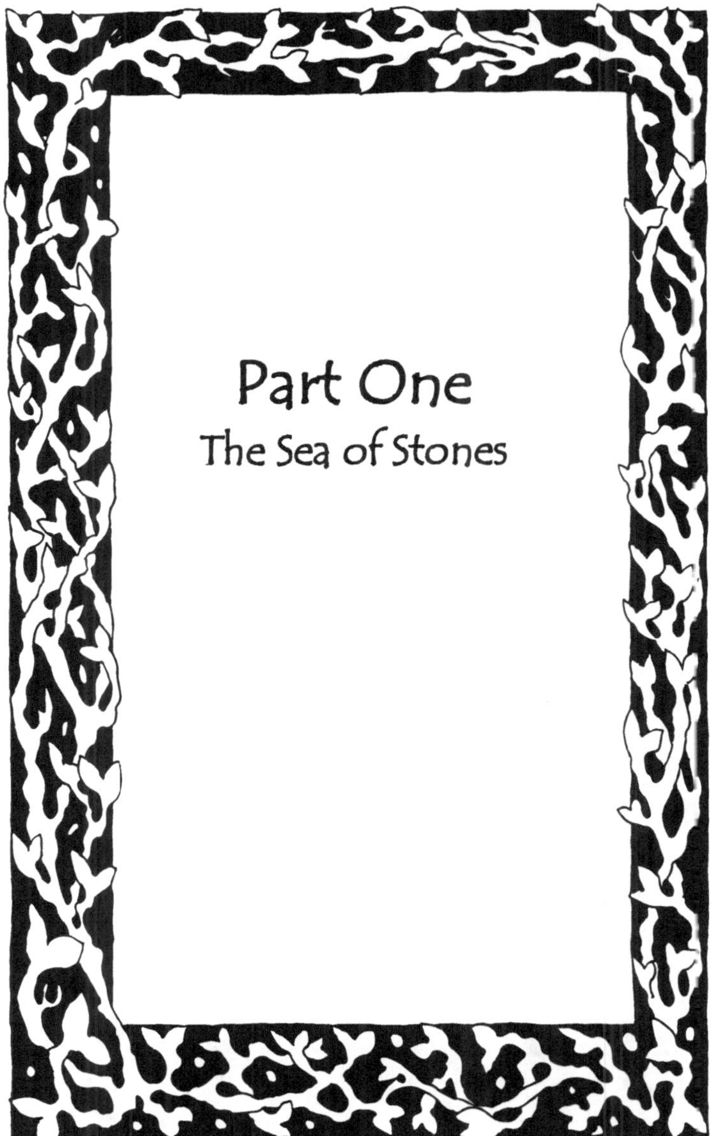

Part One
The Sea of Stones

Contents Part One

The Plant Whisperer

Inspired by the sea-thrift (*Armeria maritima*), a tough little plant that thrives in inhospitable places – like Chesil Beach.

He trudged along the top of the great beach, the sound of shifting pebbles following him at a respectful distance.

The close-woven fish basket he carried was clearly empty, its weight not pulling him off balance in the least.

The fishermen tending their boats far below, at the water's edge cocked an eye at him.

Not one of ours by no means.

Not any kind of fisherperson, for that matter, despite the basket. This was a man of a very different kidney, obviously seeking something. Some regarded him with pure curiosity, glancing up as they worked, some with an edge of hostility.

Who was he to be trudging along their beach?

But when one of the boys, picking up on these mixed reactions, took aim at the man with a catapult laden with a large pebble, his father caught the lad's eye and shook his head.

'But he's a foreigner,' said the boy, ready to argue it out.

Foreigners were fair game, weren't they?

'No,' said his father, eyeing the man's progress along the beach-top with interest, 'leave him be. He's a foreigner, but he's a friendly one I reckon.'

Meanwhile, the basket-carrier had stopped and was shading his eyes, peering down the far side of the beach. A moment later he disappeared from view with a great slithering of shingle, heading downwards.

While the boy regretted his lost target-practice, his father had the feeling that something new was about to begin.

On the landward side of the beach, the man had settled his basket upright and was industriously gathering leaves.

'Not quite right,' he murmured, peering at them short-sightedly. 'Close, but not quite the true thing. *You,* however,' he added, addressing a small pale-flowered plant with obvious affection and familiarity, 'you are the very bees-knees. You will forgive me if I borrow a few fragments from your person.'

He plucked the leaves and stems thoughtfully, careful not to uproot the plant. 'There,' he said at last, 'that leaves you plenty to grow with and gives me plenty to work with, and no harm done. I thank you from the bottom of my heart.'

The plant, a little lopsided and bald at the edges now, made no reply. It had secret buds ready to launch into action under these kinds of depredations. The man thanked it kindly again and moved on.

On such a still day the sound of his footsteps through the shingle carried up and over the beach and down to the fishermen.

'On the move again, then,' someone said.

But he didn't move very far, and soon everyone knew that the stranger was an apothecary.

'An apothe-what?' asked Jemmy Herring, fisherman of the Chesil, and a chap with an enquiring mind, as he tended his nets.

'Don't ee know what a 'pothecary is then, Jem?' said his neighbour, Robert Pierson, scornfully.

'No, I don't. But you can 'lighten me, Robin, I expect,' said Jem, calling his bluff.

'I … well … it's … ' Mr Pierson was floundering.

'It's a gent what deals in herbs and cures, o'course.' This was Jemmy's nine-year-old sibling, Annie, putting the pair of them to scorn.

Jemmy attempted a half-hearted cuff at her ear, but she was too quick for him and darted off.

'Far too 'cute for her own good, that un,' said Robert Pierson.

Jemmy nodded good-naturedly. He didn't entirely care for being put right by his little sister. Still, he would happily wager a week's catch that she'd turn out to be right; she usually was.

It was time to form an opinion, Jemmy knew. A wise man in cures was something they very much needed in this remote place on Chesil. So, this was a good thing, wasn't it? Well, answered a cautionary voice in his head, only if they are good cures, eh? Jemmy determined to find out.

The apothecary, Dr Thrift, had fetched up in many strange places in his wandering life. But few, he thought, were as strange as Chesil. Here he was, adrift on a sea of rock, an unsolid, shifting pebble-heap where the sea set the tone day and night. The heaviest waves rolled in and shook the great beach beneath him, rinsed the pebbles out whether they needed it or not, and rearranged them, never satisfied with the design. In its most cantankerous mood, the sea picked them up and hurled them. The ocean was surely a malcontent most of the time, or so Dr Thrift thought when the beach had roared and rattled all night. The sea spat out a fine mist too that hung over the beach like a pall, making everything dank and chill. It was not a place to spend the winter, he decided, and looked forward to a move inland later in the year.

But the great beach did provide him with good herbs – some scarce ones, too – and he would stay as long as the supply lasted. By winter, he knew, this place must be blasted, and the leaves browned; but for now, he worked with the plants, bidding a polite good day to sea bindweed, beet, sea campion, spurrey, and the yellow horned-poppy. He greeted them as old friends and begged a few flowers, leaves, or precious seeds for his collections.

Dr Thrift was a wary individual: slow to trust and secretive. But his was an ungreedy soul and he accepted only what he needed in return for his cures, and sometimes nothing at all. Annie Herring found this a curious way to live and asked him, with the directness of childhood, why he was so ragged and had so few possessions.

'Why,' he said, 'whatever would I do with great mounds of things to keep? It would only make me a target for bad men who would take them away again.

And besides, I am a travelling sort of person. However would I carry it all?'

Annie pointed out that if he charged the going rate for his cures he could buy a horse to ride and a mule to carry his things.

'Bless your heart,' said Dr Thrift, 'I am not a horse-riding man; they're such great heavy animals and full of wind, too. And a mule: a creature with the disposition of a bad-tempered coot. No, I travel on my own two feet with what I can carry myself, no more.'

Annie found this want of ambition a little disappointing and said so.

'Ah well,' said the apothecary, smiling, 'my ambition lies in another direction, young Annie: to be a diligent herbalist; the best I can. Is that not a better thing to work for than fine clothes and flatulent horses? Now then, you can assist me, if you will, by holding my basket for me while I gather a little – only a little – of this sea campion. Its roots can be made into soap, you know.'

Annie nodded and took the basket, having learned that Dr Thrift's apparent folly might actually be wisdom dressed up in a ragged coat.

Plants have their Secrets

Inspired by the sea arrowgrass (*Triglochin maritima*) a plant that's just about edible if you avoid the poisonous bits. It grows in areas of saltmarsh behind Chesil.

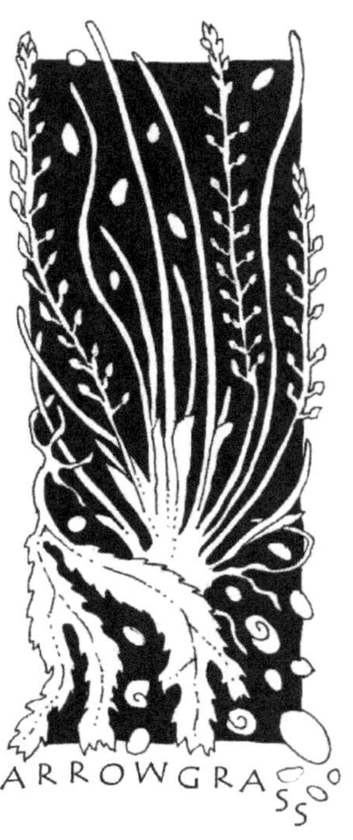

'He is a force of nature, they do say,' said Robert Pierson, with the air of somebody who knew one when he saw one. 'In every sense o' the word,' he added cryptically.

This was a step too far, and Jemmy Herring paused in folding his nets.

'Y' can't leave it at that,' said Jemmy. 'When is a force not just a force, then?'

Robert closed his eyes, a very annoying habit that warned Jemmy he was about to be instructed about something.

'In some parts, Jem, a force is what you might call a "waterfall." Gushes down a steep place and carries all with it. What I mean is, that fellow is a force, and he might wash us all away.'

Jemmy considered this awhile, his net now spread from arm to arm as if the fish might leap conveniently out of the sea and straight into it of their own volition.

'But that apothecary-man is a gentle sort o'

person,' he said at last, folding the net. 'A little curious in his habits, all that talking to the plants I mean, but he don't seem forceful at all, not to me.'

Mr Pierson tapped his nose. It was another annoying habit that he indulged in so often it was no wonder his nose seemed permanently out of joint, and said knowingly, 'We shall see, Jem, we shall see.'

A large, smooth, deep-green roller turned over lazily and broke heavily onto the beach before them, its followers widely spaced, equally large and heavy. 'It'll be coming on to blow presently, then,' said Jemmy, eyeing the surf. This was the sort of force of nature he perfectly understood, and never mind the apothecary-man.

For all that, Dr Thrift had captured Jemmy's attention and, if indeed it was about to blow, it would be a kindness to go and see that all was snug and properly battened down at the old, black fisherman's hut that the apothecary had adopted as his temporary home.

In ordinary summer weather it would be adequate for someone as un-particular about his appearance and surroundings as the good doctor. A gale might just have the roof off it though, even standing in the lee of the great beach as it did. So, Jemmy loped along with a bag of tools and set himself to finding any weak points in the structure.

Dr Thrift was heartily grateful. 'The gale will not be starting to blow this moment?' he asked, as if it might sneak over the pebbles at any time and catch him out when he wasn't looking.

'Not awhile yet, sir,' said Jemmy.

'Good. Good. Then walk with me, Mr Herring, just a little way, and show me some of the plants hereabouts.' Jemmy nodded.

'Plants have many secrets,' said Dr Thrift later, as they walked, 'and some of them are not yet known, so it's unwise to jump to conclusions.'

Jemmy was silenced; he had airily dismissed the arrowgrass plant as worthless: its flavour too bitter to eat, he knew, and he hadn't seen the doctor collect any.

The apothecary went on more kindly this time,

'Every plant has its part to play in the scheme of things, but that may not include being useful to us ... at least not yet.' He regarded the arrowgrass plant which seemed cheerfully unaware of having been grossly insulted. 'This one, for instance, may contain the cure for an ailment we have not yet encountered.'

If nothing else, Jemmy had learned never to be rude about a plant in the presence of Dr Thrift. Jemmy blew out his cheeks and attempted to change the subject. 'Tell me,' he said, 'if *we* continue to collect the herbs we do have a use for' – he had rather cleverly included himself here, he thought – 'will they not become rare and hard to find?'

'That is a good question, Mr Herring. As to the quantity *I* collect' – the apothecary put himself firmly back in charge – 'why, it is a mere drop in the ocean; I take only what I need. This is not a job for a greedy person. Yes, take only what you need, and you will generally do no harm. It's as simple as that, young sir.'

He patted the arrowgrass plant affectionately on its unattractive flowerhead and wandered on.

Reaching the Crossroads

'Everyone reaches a crossroads in their lives. Everyone. Depend upon it.'

This was one of the many things the apothecary had said as they walked, and it weighed on Jemmy Herring's mind. Perhaps this moment was Jemmy's own crossroads. The choice was simple: remain a  fisherman forever and ever amen, a mackerel-flavoured sort of life, or find a means of escape.

The mackerel-flavoured life was hard and not reliably productive, but it was familiar to Jemmy and all his forebears for time out of mind. The escape, on the other hand, was an unknown quantity: exciting, but laced with every kind of uncertainty. Jemmy peered down at his clumsy sea-boots and wondered what manner of shoes he might walk in, should he choose a mackerel-free future.

It made him dizzy to think of it; that great unknown outside world, far beyond Chesil. And what might that world contain? Jemmy knew the dangers and rewards of the sea, but a solid, unmoving, dry land sort of future was a very different matter. What might it hold for a young man with a smidgen of ambition?

Jemmy decided that, taking one thing with another, it was worth the risk. And he saw a safer way of doing it too, than simply striking out alone into the unknown. He would stick to the apothecary like a shadow from now on. He would make himself useful and learn all about the herbs and medicines; he'd employ subterfuges to do it if he must. Dr Thrift was an odd individual, no denying it, but he had experienced the outside world.

And when at last the apothecary moved on from Chesil, as he surely would, Jemmy would go with him.

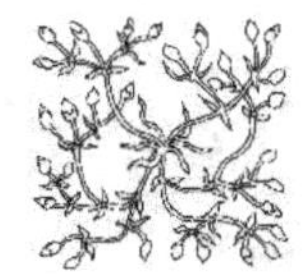

Dr Thrift's First Story

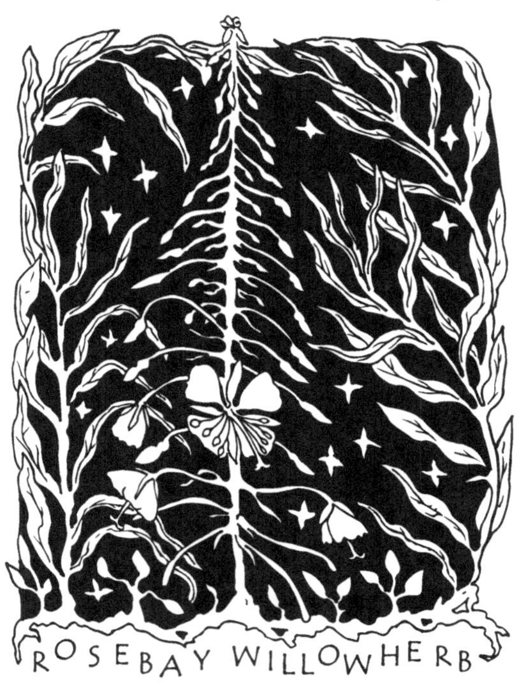

Stronger than the Stars

Inspired by the rosebay willowherb, or fireweed, (*Chamaerion angustifolium*), a plant with a spectacular blazing flowerhead.

The Chesil children gathered eagerly for an unusual event: a storytelling, and not one of those so often repeated by their mothers and grandmamas either.

'Are you ready?' asked Dr Thrift. Fifteen heads nodded as one, and none more keenly than Annie Herring's.

'Very well, this is how it begins. Once upon a time, there was a boy who was born under unfavourable stars. "The stars don't lie," people said. Wherever you go, ill-luck will follow: written in the stars, it was, day you was born. Some said the wise woman who attended his birth had stood back from his cradle, face all white, and wouldn't stay in the house with him, just in case the ill-luck made an early start.'

'That's not fair,' said Annie Herring. 'How could he help when he was born?' Everyone nodded in sympathy.

'That's just what the boy said,' Dr Thrift shook his head sadly. 'But people would never let him forget his unfortunate stars. No-one wanted him as apprentice in a decent trade; thought it might spoil their business. Only the old bargeman would take him, and the bad stars condemned him to a life carrying coals up and down the great river. A hard life it was, for a bright boy with a brain in his head.'

'So, what happened to him?' said Annie, being an interested bright girl with a brain in *her* head.

'I'm coming to that,' said Dr Thrift. 'One night, when he and the bargeman were waiting for the turn of the tide, the old man was saying, as he always did, that he hoped the boy wouldn't bring bad luck on the voyage. The boy found his courage and turned on the bargeman, said that he was going to prove he was *stronger* than the stars. A bold move, don't you think?' A bold move indeed, the children thought, and asking for a clip round the ear, too. A boy who stood up to his elders! This was turning into a very good story.

Dr Thrift read their faces. 'The bargeman was a rough sort of man, but not unkind, and he didn't punish the boy for his cheek. He merely set him to start loading the coal sacks aboard, ready to take them to the big city.'

There was a collective sigh of relief.

'They set off in the early dawn with the ebb tide, finding their way by starlight. As the heavy barge moved downstream, it seemed the stars blazed brighter than ever in the sky, which was strange seeing as it was dawn. But it was not the stars that blazed, it was the city in the distance, all aflame.'

Dr Thrift paused to let this sink in. A whole city, all on fire. It was very nearly beyond the children's imaginations.

'The bargeman hauled the tiller round, and the boy jumped ashore with a line. They secured the barge and looked on in awe as the fire raged and buildings exploded, one after another.

"Look," said the old man, "look what you've done *now*."'

The children frowned in sympathetic outrage.

Dr Thrift went on, 'The boy said it was nothing to do with him. But the bargeman insisted, as always. "Ill-starred, you are. They'll need someone to blame, look, there goes the arsenal, and you'll do as well as any. Best stay away. Besides," the old man said, regarding the laden barge, "coals is the last thing they'll be wanting just now. We'll find a buyer upstream."

"If I can cause a fire like that," said the boy, wondering at his own power, "then I can put it out again. They won't blame me, they'll thank me."

The old man looked at him askance. "Best make a start, then, lad." And down they sat, the old bargeman waiting patiently, the boy with his face screwed up in fire-stopping thought, waiting for the tide to turn again while the stars and the city blazed away.'

'Blazed away,' said Annie. 'It's a very good story, Dr Thrift, sir, but was the boy really stronger than his stars?'

'That, little Miss Herring, is a very good question,' said Dr Thrift, peering thoughtfully out to sea.

A Predatory Daisy

Inspired by the sea mayweed (*Tripleurospermum maritimum*), a plant of Chesil, which is a lot tougher than it looks.

Daisy Goodship grabbed a handful of seaweed out of the net and threw it back into the sea, with real intent to harm. I'm not getting any younger, she thought, and still not wed! Marriage was important to a girl. It gave you status: a position higher up the pecking order, and lower down the pity order. This was her twentieth summer, after all, and she knew it wouldn't be long before the pitying looks began. And what prospect of marriage was there? Why, none at present other than that fool, Jemmy Herring.

There he was again, just along the beach, staring at her in that gormless way of his. She was tempted to lob the next handful of seaweed straight into his face.

Was he really the best she could do?

Instinct had made her look at every boy and man in the village with a degree of interest. She knew them all too well; that was the trouble. She had even cast an appraising eye over that apothecary fellow, odd though he was. Off-comers were scarce, and this one called himself a *doctor*, no less. Life as a doctor's wife would certainly be a step up from a career as Mrs Jemmy

Herring. But what kind of a living did a man make from selling cures, the ever-practical Daisy wondered? Not much of one, to judge by the scruffy state of him. And no wonder, really, when the apothecary gave away his herbs for nothing to those who couldn't pay. Or said they couldn't. She'd soon put a stop to *that* nonsense, if only he'd cast an eye in her direction. She'd smarten him up to a state befitting a doctor, too.

Daisy tried flirting, batting her eyelashes, and visiting the apothecary for small cures she didn't need, just to be alone with him. But he had shown no more interest in her than if she had been a squid with a broken tentacle. Indeed, the squid would have been better placed to get his attention.

Perhaps, she thought, he just isn't the marrying kind, and returned her thoughts to the problem of the gormless Jemmy. There was really no choice, not with time running short: Jemmy Herring would have to do. Daisy found excuses to be wherever he was and baited her traps with smiles. She said nothing at all to Jemmy himself, but airily let it be known to everyone else that she and he were stepping out.

Daisy's seductive powers were limited, but since Jemmy seemed to be taking the bait anyway, she reckoned she wouldn't be needing them. Once there was a child on the way there would be a good-natured enforced wedding and her future would be secured. The poor fool would scarcely have felt the net closing around him.

And Jemmy wasn't the sort of man to need much knocking into shape: he was a hard worker and pretty honest after all. Good enough, she supposed. There was only one thing that troubled her: the amount of time he spent with Dr Thrift. Jemmy followed him around like a spaniel pup: always at the apothecary's heels, hanging on his every word. Very strange, and she couldn't make out the reason for it. She did perceive it as a threat, though. The very moment she had a ring on her finger, Jemmy's visits to Dr Thrift were going to come to an abrupt end; that much was for certain.

Stone and Bone

Inspired by the sea pea (*Lathyrus japonicus*). It grows directly on the Chesil shingle.

From the landward side of the beach, the soft sound of the apothecary's voice had gone on for quite a while. Jemmy Herring found it soothing: that steady flow of words, occasionally punctuated with chuckles, as if the plants were talking back to him in an amiable way. Jemmy idly wondered if it might indeed be possible to hold conversations with herbs and was just thinking he might try passing the time of day with a sea kale the next time he met one, when there was a silence. Quite a prolonged and unusual silence from the other side of the beach; Jemmy looked up and listened intently. Nothing.

'This is strange,' he said aloud, as if to fill the sudden quiet. 'The 'pothecary talks all the time to his plants when he's out collecting.'

He listened a while longer, but not a word floated back, and no sound of someone trudging through the pebbles. So, he must still be there.

Jemmy began the steep climb up from the waterline, scattering shingle, but paused halfway, just to see if the customary talk had resumed. It had not, so he clambered on towards the crest of the beach.

Stopping at the top to catch his breath, he found there was a new sound: not talking but sobbing. The apothecary was kneeling in the shingle a few yards down, his face streaming with tears. He looked up at Jemmy and said, 'Oh, Mr Herring, it is the very pity of the world. See, it is a dead mermaid.'

Jemmy didn't hold with mermaids and such, but all the same, he touched the shark's tooth he wore on a bootlace around his neck for luck and protection against evil; a fisherman needed all the help he could get. Thus fortified, he slithered down for a proper look at the corpse, which lay on a bed of sea-pea.

'Oh, no, sir,' he said, patting the apothecary on the shoulder. 'No mermaid. That's a dolphin baby, still smiling, see? This ol' beach, sir, is made of stone and bone, y'know, of all the creatures that washes up out of the sea. That's why it seems like it's 'live sometimes.'

Dr Thrift blew his nose and composed himself. 'Of course, of course,' he said. 'Forgive me. Such foolishness. Oh, and don't eat those peas, will you. Very bad.'

It wasn't the first time the apothecary had shown a whimsical side to his nature. It wasn't a good look for a herbalist. Jemmy knew he should have been a little concerned by it, but in all truth, his mind was too much distracted by another matter to pay much attention.

Dr Thrift's Second Story

Ill-gotten Gains

Inspired by the scattered gold of lesser celandine (*Ficaria verna*), visible in every hedgerow and woodland in the springtime.

The Chesil children gathered eagerly when Dr Thrift announced he would be telling another story.

'Is this one about the stars again?' asked Annie Herring.

'No,' said Dr Thrift. 'This one concerns gold.'

This was a promising topic, so Annie said no more.

'Once upon a time,' said Dr Thrift, settling down, 'there were two brothers. One day they were out in the forest, gathering firewood, when they saw something shining in a mossy gap under an oak root.'

None of the children had ever seen an oak tree, not here on the desolate Chesil, and it seemed a satisfyingly exotic setting for a story.

'The brothers crouched and looked. Reached out to touch and then sat back on their heels.

"Is that gold?" asked the elder brother.'

'Real gold?' Annie couldn't resist interrupting. 'I wonder how it came to be there?'

'Real gold,' said Dr Thrift, nodding, 'and that is just what the brothers wondered, too. The younger brother, who fancied himself the wiser man, pulled out a single, large beautiful coin, considered a moment and then said he thought it was old. Maybe hidden in the days of the old North-Men. Ill-gotten gains. The elder brother, a greedy young man, reckoned it was their gold now, whoever it had belonged to. But before they could dig it out, they heard someone approaching. The two concealed themselves behind a holly bush, as if even the thought of theft rendered them guilty.

"Oh," whispered the elder brother, peering out. "It is a great magpie, big as a man. It is *his* cache of shiny things. He'll peck our eyes out!"

The younger brother shushed him. "You're such a fool. That is no magpie, you pea-brain; it's a man in a black and white cloak.'"

The children laughed at this foolishness, but Dr Thrift went on, 'Magpie or no, the man knew of the golden hoard in the tree root and stooped to inspect it. The younger brother watched and saw with dismay that the beautiful coin was still in his hand. He dropped it, not wishing to be accused of theft. The flash of its movement showed through the darkness of the holly bush and the cloaked stranger turned his beady black eyes upon the brothers. They froze, squeezing their own eyes shut in terror, shocking cowards really. The elder brother opened first one eye, experimentally, and then both. The magpie man had gone. But when they crept out and returned to the oak root there was no sign of the gold, either. The younger brother picked up the coin he had dropped and slipped it into his pocket secretly, saying not a word to the elder brother.

Neither of them noticed that high above, in the ragged branches of the oak, a magpie was setting up a furious chatter of curses.'

Annie sought to clarify: 'So the man in the cloak turned himself into a magpie?'

'Very astute,' said Dr Thrift. 'He was a conjuror with many powers. It was an unwise move to steal his gold, don't you agree?'

Annie nodded. Very unwise.

Love and Parsnips

Inspired by the wild parsnip (*Pastinaca sativa*), a herb, with curative properties that grows all along Chesil Beach.

Jemmy Herring looked at the unhappy mackerel in his hand and hesitated. He tried so hard not to think of Daisy, but there she was again, invading his thoughts. Women: they were an entrapment, sure enough. And Jemmy didn't want to end up like his own father: not unhappy, exactly, but weighted down with a wife and nine hungry children. The responsibility, the incessant demands. Mr Herring, senior, had been *so* weighted with it all that when his boat sank, he was taken straight down to the seabed, and permanent rest, without much of a struggle.

Jemmy didn't fancy *that*, but he did fancy Daisy. He couldn't say why, not entirely. She wasn't exceptionally pretty, but still his brain remained stubbornly full of her. And oh, her image was everywhere. He saw it in the startled expressions of the mackerel as he hauled them in; he saw her in the sinuous tentacles and goggling eyes of the squid; the snapping claws of a trapped crab brought her directly to mind.

She is a nice enough girl, said Jemmy's rational mind, *but she is a trap for the unwary too, and especially for me. I must not think of her.*

But hard as he tried, the sneaky Daisy was always waiting, seeking an unguarded moment, or the reminding face of a passing mackerel, to put a foot in the door of his thoughts, pry it open, and take up residence once again.

Jemmy sighed, took pity on the gasping fish, and threw it back into the sea. Proof positive, if it were needed, that he was no longer in his right mind.

'You should have a care with the wild parsnips, you know,' said Dr Thrift. 'Not a herb to be trifled with, and possibly dangerous to the constitution.'

'What d' ye mean?' said Jemmy Herring, pausing in his digging-up of roots. 'Surely the parsnip is a wholesome plant, everyone eats them. What's so dangerous?'

Dr Thrift shook his head. 'Your garden parsnip is no threat, Mr Herring. Wholesome, as you say. But these here are wildlings, different in many degrees. Now, tell me why you are digging them.'

Jemmy went on the defensive. 'I heard tell they can cure me of love,' he said miserably, 'chopped roots, mashed with squid eyes, three times a day after meals. That's what they say. Then I won't think of her, never again.' He folded his arms tightly, daring the apothecary to argue.

'Well,' said Dr Thrift, scratching his head, 'love is a disease of sorts, and it may be curable. But not with wild parsnips, Mr Herring. They will merely give you the wind and a nasty rash, I fear. Come with me and I will make you a herbal concoction, something more dainty and delicate that will ease your mind, but without the unfortunate side effects.'

And with that, he trudged off across the shingle towards the tumbledown hut that served as the apothecary-shop. Jemmy followed and wondered just how much this wonderful medicine was going to cost him. Perhaps, he thought, I should risk the wild parsnips after all.

'Now then, Mr Herring, would you care to tell me a little more?' Dr Thrift was busy mixing with a pestle and mortar. 'I can create a tailor-made potion for you if I fully understand the problem.'

'The problem is called Daisy Goodship,' said Jemmy, thinking he had nothing to lose by being candid.

'Ah,' said the apothecary, feeling along the shelf for a bottle and finding it without even taking his eye off the pestle and mortar. 'The lovely Miss Goodship. Now, that is a young lady in search of a husband, I think.'

'How d' ye know about that?' asked Jemmy.

'Well,' said Dr Thrift, now pounding the dried leaves of something, 'she has cast her nets wide, shall we say. Even so far as myself.'

Daisy had looked at the apothecary? *His* Daisy? Jemmy caught himself with the intention of punching the good doctor on the nose. He mastered himself, took a seat on a rickety stool, and thought it through. They *both* needed to escape Daisy's clutches, particularly if the anti-love potion was unsuccessful. This was an advantage, Jemmy saw, and he determined to redouble his efforts to make himself useful to the apothecary.

Dr Thrift's Third Story

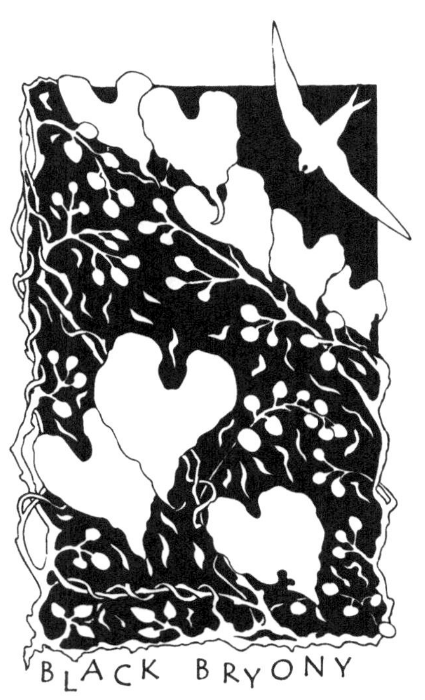

The Devil-bird

Inspired by the black bryony (*Tamus communis*), a hedgerow plant, both beautiful and poisonous.

All the children begged for another story. The apothecary, Dr Thrift, told such excellent tales. They were just the right length and had just the right degree of menace. But there was nothing so real you would lose sleep over it.

'Very well,' said the apothecary. 'A salutary tale, then.' The children settled to listen, wondering what "salutary" might mean. 'There was once a man who would gather poison berries from the hedges. The ones he preferred were from the black bryony plant, red and luscious.' He stopped, regarding the children sternly. 'They have their uses, but not to be eaten though, oh dear, no. Never. But you know that, of course.'

The children nodded eagerly, though none of them had ever seen a bryony plant.

'Yes,' said the apothecary, 'to be sure. Well. Here was a man, gathering his berries one pleasant September day, when he was interrupted by a loud shriek. He thought, just for a moment, that the plant, a magical species, as you know, had taken exception to the theft of its berries and found a voice with which to object. Had its root hurled itself out of the ground and thrown a tantrum like a mandrake, beating its little fists on the ground? Well, no. In the first place, he didn't, in all common sense, think that was possible, and in the second place, the shriek had come from above his head. The bryony was not to blame, the culprit was a devil-bird.' Dr Thrift paused again. 'A swift. You see them here, don't you?'

Everyone agreed that yes, there were devil-birds here every summer, nesting under the eaves.

'But not in September,' somebody said, 'they all be gone by then.'

'Exactly so, very good.' said the apothecary. 'That is just what the berry-gatherer thought: very late for a devil-bird and a thought is what it should have stayed. "You are out of season, Mr Swift," he said, quite jovial, to the bird circling above. The swift snarled and swooped around his very ears and said, "That's as maybe, but it will be open season on you, sir, if you stick your nose into what's none of your business."

The apothecary stopped again and stared along the great shingle bank. The children looked at each other. 'So, what did the berry-gatherer do, sir?'

Dr Thrift came out of his reverie. 'Why, what do you think he did? Dropped his basket of berries and ran for his life, of course.'

The children agreed that being verbally threatened by a snarling bird justified a certain amount of running away. 'But really,' they asked, 'what could a bird that size actually do to you?'

The apothecary shook his head, unusually impatient. 'No, not a bird, don't you see? Not even a devil-bird. A magical creature, most malevolent and vengeful.'

He had become so solemn that the children moved away, nearly jumping out of their skins when an innocent party of swifts went screaming joyfully overhead.

Essence of Storksbill

Inspired by Common Storksbill (*Erodium cicutarium*), very much a woman's plant, providing various herbal remedies for nursing mothers. It grows commonly on the shingle of Chesil.

'Why isn't God married, Ma?' Annie Herring had set her chin, stubbornly demanding an answer.

Her mother paused in her sweeping and faced the child.

'What sort of a question is that?'

'The 'pothecary says it's the kind of question we should all ask,' said Annie. 'He tells us things.' She could see her mother was rattled and was rather enjoying it.

'What things?' Mrs Herring frowned. This smacked of heresy or witchcraft, or possibly both. What business had the apothecary, putting this sort of dangerous nonsense into children's heads?

'Oh,' said Annie, scuffing her foot on the floor and making the dust fly again, 'just things. And stories about talking animals. Says we should ask questions if we don't know things.'

Her mother turned on her, pointing the broom handle into her face for emphasis. 'You keep away from the 'pothecary, Annie Herring, 'cept for medicinal purposes only. And don't you go asking such questions of anyone else, specially not the parson, or I'll have the hide off you.'

Annie knew the threat of a beating was probably a bluff, but she took a step away from the broom handle anyway. 'Yes, Ma,' she said quietly, hanging her head and looking up through her eyelashes; that usually worked.

'Yes. Well,' said her mother, softening, and lowering the broom. 'I blame the 'pothecary, putting such thoughts in your head. He's a bad man. Now, off with you.'

Annie skipped out. Was the apothecary really a bad man, as her mother said? She thought not; he mends people, and animals, he talks to the plants. Tells us such stories, too. Besides, nobody is all good or all bad, all greedy or all generous, all clever or all stupid. Everyone was made up of all sorts of bits and pieces. And you never knew which side you would see next. Annie was having her first philosophical thought, although she didn't know it; the first of many. However, she did know she would be defying her mother and going back to see the apothecary again. She'd just be a little more circumspect about it. So there.

She also knew she'd learned something far more important than why it was that God didn't happen to be married.

The Benefit of Cures

Inspired by the Tree Mallow (*Lavatera arborea*), whose leaves can be made into a poultice to treat sprains. Grows on sand and shingle behind Chesil.

When Mrs Herring took a breather from her many chores, it was her habit to lean over the garden wall and complain about her children to her neighbours.

On this particular day, the only available audience was the man next door. He was an ancient and desiccated article, who had taken up poisonous gossip as a hobby since his retirement from the fishing trade. He was in a particularly nasty mood, too, having fallen and sprained his ankle. Mrs Herring knew it was unwise to share confidences with him; it was more entertaining, and safer, to simply listen.

Today, his chosen subject for demolition was the apothecary. That dedicated and skilful gent would have been horrified had he heard.

'Talks to carrots, you know. The wild 'uns, not the eating kind. Madder than a hatter in a lead mine. Creeps about conversationalising with herbs. Now, Mrs Herring, would you entrust your life to someone who carries on like that?'

Mrs Herring began to nod, and then shook her head in confusion. She had already entrusted her life to one of the apothecary's cures, and that of her youngest child, too. 'But the cures do seem to work.' she said doubtfully. Indeed, she was pretty sure Dr Thrift would have something to treat the sprain.

Her neighbour frowned and said confidentially, 'Don't you do it, Mrs Herring, you take my tip. We's all in thrall to a madman. 'Cepting me, of course. I wouldn't let him touch a hair of my chin nor a single bunion neither, that apothecary fellow.' He dropped his voice further and she leaned in to hear. 'They say he turns hisself into aminals after dark. That's what they say.'

Mrs Herring turned to look at her line of washing a moment, while she thought. Hadn't her Annie said something about talking animals? She turned back to ask for more details, but the old fellow had limped painfully off, content that he had planted the seeds of discord.

So, was the apothecary a good addition to the community or not? There was the benefit of the cures on the good side, but there was all this encouraging of children to ask awkward questions on the bad side. Somewhere in the middle there was a rather strange individual who talked to plants.

Mrs Herring wasn't the only one left confused. Annie Herring had her theories about Dr Thrift. They kept her mind occupied while she was gutting the fish. He was such an exotic sort of gentleman and said such unexpected things; he could surprise you over and over.

'It's the stories, you see,' she said to herself, flinging a disembowelled mackerel into the barrel. 'I

think they are his true history, and not made up at all.'
It was a bold thought.

She went over the stories: *the boy who made the city catch fire, surely someone with magical powers; the gold in the tree-root, and the magpie; the swift that threatened people. Ah, yes, the magical creatures! Had he really dealt with magical creatures? Was he able to turn himself into magical creatures? That was it! The stories were true, but Dr Thrift himself wasn't the victim of magical creatures; he became the magical creatures.* Annie paused, enjoying the detective work, doomed mackerel in hand.

'You're wool-gathering, child,' said her mother's voice. 'Get on with it, now.'

Annie complied, but was still thinking it through. She needed to share her suspicions with someone. Her mother would certainly not be sympathetic, that much was certain. But Jemmy would listen if he weren't mooning too much over that Daisy Goodship. Her brother was a soft touch where his little sister was concerned. He was easily led, and she was sharp enough to know it. Annie's plan began to form; she would go and sit with him when he was mending the nets, set out her theories, and see what he had to say. He was indulgent enough to listen, and kind enough not to make fun of her. She tackled the next unlucky fish with gusto, her mind made up.

But Dr Thrift still had another story to tell.

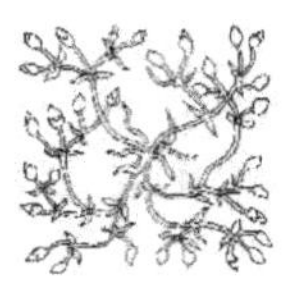

Dr Thrift's Fourth Story

FLEABANE

A Singular Ringlet

Inspired by the common fleabane (*Pulicaria dysenterica*), a plant once used to deter insect pests. Strangely enough, butterflies love the flowers.

The children gathered, as before, and fell quiet; especially Annie, who was paying the closest attention.

'Once upon a time,' said the apothecary, 'there was a man who wandered the forest, and very happy he was there, too. He searched the woods for herbs and there were many to discover, so many cures for all ailments. That's how he made his living: gall stones, madam? Bunions? The blue ague? He had the remedies and sold them at fair prices to the people he met, along with truthful assessments of how much improvement might be expected. He was not a quack, you see.'

'Oh, Dr Thrift,' somebody said, 'surely this is you? Are you telling a story about yourself?'

'No,' said the apothecary, 'it was told to me by a friend. Now, shall we go on?'

Everyone nodded.

'Well,' said the apothecary, picking up the thread, 'one day this good herbalist met a butterfly, a ringlet, which is a dark sort of butterfly with little iron-coloured rings underneath its wings.'

'That there is silly,' said one of the children. 'How can you *meet* a butterfly?'

'Any more interruptions,' said Dr Thrift, 'and I shall go and do something else instead.'

Annie shushed the inquisitive child. They were putting him off.

'Very well. The butterfly wished him a good morning, as you do. He was surprised, but not all that surprised, having dealt with talking creatures once or twice before. It's not as uncommon as you might expect. "I've been looking for you," said the insect, in a matter-of-fact tone. "I saw what you did, you know." The herbalist blustered at the creature, "You're nothing but a mangy insect. What would you know about anything?" The butterfly flapped its ragged wings, so the iron rings seemed to rattle together and said again, more menacing this time, "I know who you are, and I saw what you did!"

Well, now. The herbalist was afraid.'

'As you would be,' said somebody at the back. 'There's naught so terrifying as being threatened by a cabbage white!'

'Not a cabbage white; a ringlet. I've told you about interruptions,' said the apothecary in exasperation. 'Now, do you want to hear the story or not?'

Everyone went quiet again.

'Yes, well. As I said, the herbalist was afraid, not of the butterfly, even a talking one, but because he did indeed have a guilty secret; he feared the ringlet might have found it out. So, he searched in his bag of herbs and cures, seeking his stash of fleabane, which, when properly used, is a highly effective insecticide … '

'He set out to murder the butterfly, then!'

'Who's telling this story, eh?' said Dr Thrift. 'That's it, one interruption too many.'

'But what about the guilty secret?' Someone called out.

'You don't deserve to hear it,' said the apothecary and stormed off, leaving waves of indignation in his wake; none so indignant as Annie Herring, who desperately wanted to know any guilty secrets that might be available for disclosure.

Colic and Garlic

Inspired by the crow garlic (*Allium vineale*) which was once used as a herb to treat colic in children, and grows among grass behind Chesil.

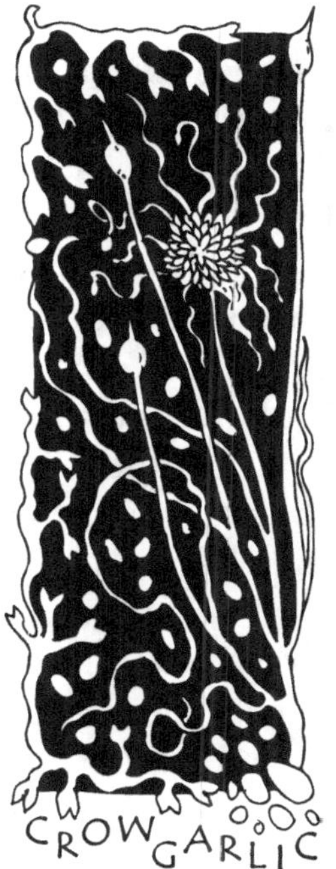

Net-mending was always a contemplative time for Jemmy Herring. The work was largely automatic and he could ruminate at will, chew over the mysteries of life in the safety of his own head, but not today. Today, his head was full of Daisy Goodship, despite the doctor's anti-love potion, and very unwelcome she was too. Jemmy sincerely wished she would vacate the premises forthwith. He needed a distraction, and when Annie sidled up to him he was glad of the respite.

'Jem,' she said, tentatively, 'do you think the 'pothecary is ... might be ... a magician?'

Jemmy would have patted her on the head had his hands not been full of net. 'Bless your heart, no,' he said, looking at her closely. She had a pained look about her, he thought. A touch of colic, maybe? He had been paying attention to the way Dr Thrift dealt with his patients, and it was tempting to make a diagnosis or two for himself. She glared at him and he went on. 'For sure, he's a learned man, good with the cures, but that don't make him magical, do it?'

Annie persisted. 'Not the cures, Jem. The stories. I think the stories he tells are real; about *him*, and not made up at all.'

Jemmy put the net down this time and turned to his sister. 'Whatever makes you say that Baby-Annie?'

The regression to this childish nickname was annoying, but Annie ignored it. 'Some of them are about herbalists and he's a herbalist.' It sounded so lame, spoken aloud like that.

Jemmy took up his net again. 'Well, he knows about herbs, stands to reason he would tell stories about them. Doesn't mean they're about him.'

This was so wise and logical that Annie fell quiet for a moment and then said, 'Or, they *are* about him, but he 'broiders them with magic creatures to make it more interesting.'

Jemmy smiled, all brotherly indulgence. 'Well, there you are, young Annie. I 'spect that's just what he does, too. I think you got a touch o' the colic, maybe. We'll ask the doctor for a herb for you, shall we?'

'Oh, no! He'll make me eat the garlic cure,' said Annie in dismay, and darted off. She had been paying attention, too.

But the things Annie had said lingered about Jemmy's mind. If she were right, and he wasn't saying she was, his future appeared ever more exciting. Not just apprentice to an apothecary, apprentice to a magician! It was dangerous, it was powerful, it was thrilling. And it knocked the spots off the dull future he so dreaded. It was the stuff of dreams.

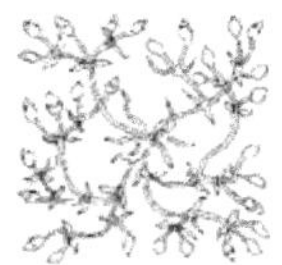

Part Two
Flotsam and Jetsam

Contents Part Two

The Restless Season

Inspired by sea holly (*Eryngium maritimum*), a plant with many herbal uses and many prickly leaves.

When the plants began to pack themselves away for the winter: when the flamboyant flowers of the thyme were long gone and it was nothing but a dwindling green mat, and when late summer tranquillity was replaced by a fresher, more practical season, Dr Thrift the apothecary began to pack up his things too. The dried herbs that had festooned the rafters of his dark hut on the beach were taken down and carefully sorted into little bags, each bearing a mysterious symbol. Jemmy pretended to others that he understood these symbols, but in reality he had only the haziest idea that they were astrological and related to which planet ruled which plant.

He marvelled at the apothecary's knowledge, at how much abstract information the man kept in his skull. Jemmy's own limited knowledge left him unsure at times regarding the boundaries between herbalism, alchemy, and plain, old-fashioned witchcraft. It was an exciting line of work though, perched as it was, between the power it gave the apothecary over people and the ever-present danger of being accused of blasphemy.

Jemmy sensed there was a deadline at work,

possibly just seasonal, but possibly something more urgent. This was confirmed, at least in Jemmy's mind, when the good doctor stabbed himself on an obstreperous sea holly leaf and uttered a rude word; the first Jemmy had ever heard him use.

Some people had begged Dr Thrift to stay, notably young Annie Herring. Others would be glad to see the back of him, notably Annie's mother.

Jemmy, increasingly anxious, made himself as useful as possible, assisting with the packing whenever he could and trying to learn the symbols. He was looking for the right moment to ask if he might accompany the apothecary when he left but was afraid to ask. What if the answer was no?

So, when Dr Thrift shook his head fretfully and muttered, 'Oh dear, oh dear, I don't know what I shall do without you to help, Mr Herring,' Jemmy seized the opportunity.

'Then I will come with you.' He hadn't meant to blurt it out so forcefully or so loudly, but the idea had evolved so long in his head that he couldn't stop himself.

Dr Thrift jumped back, so suddenly that he collided with the table and sent a carefully arranged stack of little herb bags flying. 'Oh dear, oh dear,' he said. 'Such frightful disorder.'

Jemmy rushed to pick up the bags and began to sort them, but the symbols swam before his eyes. He had come crashing in like a conger eel in a strop and had ruined everything with his over-enthusiasm.

Dr Thrift fussed over his scattered necropolis of plants, talking to them even in death. 'No, no, not there;

you are a herb of Mars, you see, and *you* of Jupiter. Keep yourselves to yourselves if you please.'

Jemmy's face fell. It had been mere fancy on his part to think he might escape his life with the fisherfolk. His destiny was mackerel-shaped and Daisy Goodship-shaped, and that was that.

'I'm sorry, Dr Thrift,' he said awkwardly, 'if I startled you.'

'No, no,' said the apothecary, still disentangling the muddle of herbs. 'No apologies needed, Mr Herring. Mere accident, could happen to anyone, no harm done, not really. Is there?' He addressed this last remark to a packet of thyme leaves, then he turned back to Jemmy. 'Tell me, when can you be ready to leave?'

Jemmy gaped like a codfish for a moment, collected himself, and said, 'Now. Straight away, sir, if you want me to.'

The Wreck of the Haresfoot

Inspired by the haresfoot clover (*Trifolium arvense*), a plant of the sandy turf behind Chesil.)

Before Dr Thrift could untangle his herbs, or Jemmy Herring his wits, the Chesil weather intervened very rudely. The storm that blew in on the equinox ensured, as storms so often do, that they reconsidered their priorities.

An unhappy ship, the barque *Haresfoot*, had been blown onto the beach by the pitiless gale, and concentrated the minds of all the Chesil folk, though perhaps not in the direction one might expect.

'It would be a charitable action to help them, would it not?' This was such an understatement that people took whole moments to stop and stare at the apothecary. This was time that would have been better spent in gathering up the coal that was being washed out of the ship's hold and hurled ashore in the surf like so many great black hailstones. It was forming a dark rim along the limit of the waves' reach and people were taking considerable risks to get at it. This was not as heartless as it seems: the weather and the ship being placed as they were would have made any rescue attempts pure suicide. Selflessness is a great thing, but not when it leaves orphans in its wake.

'We should help them get ashore. Can we help them?' The apothecary spoke with true concern.

'Yes,' people said, 'she's close enough in now. We can, and we should, of course we should.' So, they left the valuable coal to knock itself to pieces in the surf and began to seek ways to get a line aboard the stricken ship, to assist the small crew, all of them plainly visible and hanging on grimly. They had long since ceased worrying about preserving the cargo and were now absorbed in preserving themselves. So, a line to the shore would be a welcome thing and not before time at all.

Dr Thrift, knowing he would be more hindrance than help in the rescue itself, hurried back to his dark hut on the landward side of the beach, and began unpacking useful medicines for any survivors: yarrow for cuts and bruises, comfrey poultices for broken bones, and a bottle of painkiller; his own mixture. He took a thoughtful swig of this painkiller as he gathered everything into a bag.

'Dr Thrift! Three souls ashore and one in a bad way.' Jemmy sang out. 'Please come along, sir.'

The apothecary hurried out to do what he could.

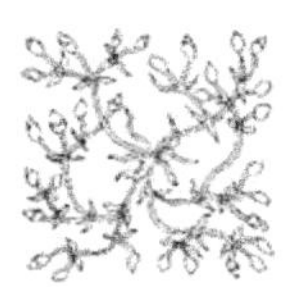

Bitter Herb

Inspired by wormwood (*Artemisia absinthium*), a very bitter herb that grows in the salt marshes behind Chesil. It is also an ingredient of absinthe, thought to cause hallucinations in drinkers.

As the *Haresfoot*, an unlucky ship despite her name, ground herself apart on the pitiless beach, Dr Thrift trudged through the shingle with the faithful Jemmy carrying his bag. They found two sailors warming before the fire in Mrs Herring's house, but the third one seemed to have been mislaid.

'He was here. Gone to report the loss o' the ship, I think.' said Mrs Herring. 'Said he were never going to sea again: never no more, no how; and rolled off as fast as his ungrateful legs would carry 'im. Never even said "thank-you-kindly."'

'Understandable in the circumstances, I suppose.' said Dr Thrift, as he examined his two remaining patients.

Mrs Herring sniffed, equally disgusted at the ingratitude and the necessity of having the apothecary in her house. But this was an emergency, so she said no more and left him to it.

The apothecary turned back to the sailors: one shattered arm, apparently incurred during the rescue operation, the man accepting the likely loss of it; the other was pale and silent, making the apothecary suspect grave internal injuries.

'Spar fell on that 'un,' said Jemmy, ever the practical sea-goer. 'Not much hope, sir, I 'magine.'

Dr Thrift shook his head slightly. 'I can ease his pain,' he murmured, taking the stoppered bottle out of his bag and handing it to Mrs Herring, adding, 'give him this wormwood extract; all of it if necessary.'

He turned to investigate the broken arm, which belonged to a true stoic. 'Caught tight in a rope, sir,' he said, managing a smile. 'Will you take it off now?'

Dr Thrift returned the smile. 'I am not a surgeon, alas,' he said, 'but I will try to set the bone before we send for the butcher, eh?'

The sailor laughed. 'Whatever you can do, sir, I'll be grateful.'

The apothecary fished in his bag for another bottle. 'This is comfrey, knitbone as they call it. We'll put a poultice over the break. Miss Annie, will you assist me?'

Jemmy felt a stab of jealousy: here he was, all ready to help, and the doctor had asked his little sister instead. He calmed himself with the thought that poultices were surely women's work, confirmed a moment later when the apothecary added, 'Mr Herring, hold the gentleman steady, if you will, while I feel for the break.'

The unlucky sailor who had got in the way of the falling spar fell feverish. He took all of the apothecary's painkiller, insisted the ship had been pushed ashore by a great black whale, then he died quietly during the night. His shipmate laughed at the notion of a whale, but admitted he had been below decks at the time, trying to secure the cargo.

'Could a whale have injured the ship?' Dr Thrift asked Jemmy.

'We don't see 'em along Chesil, sir – only dolphins. But you'd need a great weight o' *them* to sink a barque. I 'spect it was your pain-killing draught that disturbed his wits.'

Jemmy had tried a nip of it when the apothecary wasn't looking and had seen a few odd things himself when he went outside for a breath of air, including, he fancied, a seagull that had wished him good day. In the light of that, Annie's reports of the apothecary's odd tales of talking animals began to make more sense; more sense, regretfully, than the possibility of magical explanations. Perhaps Dr Thrift indulged in the stuff himself.

'I daresay you are right,' said Dr Thrift, regarding the empty bottle. 'It is a strong mixture, but it eased his passing, poor soul.'

When all had been attended to, the apothecary asked the man with the broken arm, who was bearing up well under the good influence of the poultice, about the missing sailor.

'He were the first mate, sir, and since he come ashore all safe, I guess the good lady were right and he just went to report the loss, sir, by land.' The sailor shook his head as if this were unthinkable. 'But there won't be much left of the poor ship by now, I don't think, 'cepting the coal.'

'No,' said Dr Thrift peering out of Mrs Herring's salt-caked window at the austere line of the great beach. 'But I believe the people hereabouts will collect up what they can.'

Annie Herring, listening intently at the door, then ran off to report this unguarded comment to Jemmy.

Rattled

Inspired by the yellow rattle
(*Rhinanthus*), a semi-parasitic
plant that grows among grass
behind Chesil.

It took a great deal to rattle the Chesil fishermen, but the man dressed all in black worried them. His clothes were spotless: boots polished, hat properly brushed; no worn patches, no down-at-heelness. Anybody would attract attention dressed like that. No-one here had anything that fancy, or that *new*. People stopped to stare at this weird and alien being. It was rumoured that he had been seen speaking quietly with Dr Thrift. The Chesil fisherfolk thought he was a spy from the outside world, from the far outside world. Some of them thought the same of Dr Thrift, and that the two might be in cahoots. But then such a closed community as theirs did love to dramatise the arrival of a stranger whenever they possibly could.

Jemmy Herring would have none of this. 'A true spy,' he said, 'would have dressed to blend in with the background. Them fine clothes show up wherever he goes. He's nothing but a crony of the apothecary come to visit. Besides, what do we have here that's worth spying on, eh?'

'In cahoots, them two there,' people said, stubbornly.

'What in the world is there for them to be in cahoots about that would concern us?' said Jemmy indignantly. In truth, he was jealous of this man for monopolising the apothecary's attention. It was interfering with his own carefully laid plan to learn the cures by stealth.

'The cargo, y' fool,' somebody hissed. 'The coal we took from the wreck, of course. As we should not have, as y' well know. That sailor as was unharmed went off to report the wreck, didn't he? And *this* fellow has the look of a coal merchant's man, don' he, all in black? Making 'quiries concerning the lost cargo. Stands to reason. And that 'pothecary man will betray us, a' purpose or not. They will take all that good coal away from us. And whose need is the greater, hey? We'll freeze come the winter.'

'The apothecary is a good man,' said Jemmy stoutly. 'He'd not betray us. And that is just a friend of his, come to visit, no more. Why, he's no more a spy than that there black-back gull.'

The bird gave them a quizzical look and flew lazily off along the shoreline.

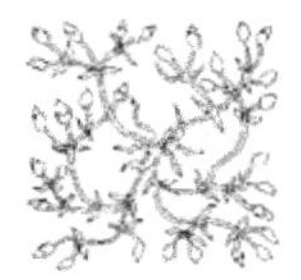

In a Bind

Inspired by sea bindweed
(*Calystegia soldanella*), which grows
on the Chesil shingle.

'Oh, Mr Herring,' said the apothecary, flapping about the hut in a fever of anxiety, and throwing things into bags. 'Oh, dear. I believe I can trust you?'

Dr Thrift didn't sound too sure, but Jemmy nodded stoutly. *Of course*, he could be trusted.

'What's the matter, sir?'

'Ah, I am a fugitive, you see.'

Jemmy wasn't sure he did see. This was stretching his vocabulary to its limit. 'A fugi … ?'

'Oh, that is to say … I must fly,' said the apothecary, distractedly.

Fly? Jemmy's staunch expression vanished, and his mouth fell open. What had Annie said? About the apothecary's magical powers, about his being able to turn into winged creatures, birds, and butterflies? For a moment, Jemmy's romantic dream of being apprenticed to a magician re-flourished.

Dr Thrift stopped long enough to pick up Jemmy's confused look. 'I am running away,' he said. 'I must.'

Jemmy's mouth fell open further as understanding increased. Running away? Not magical then? Just afraid of someone?

Jemmy was furious, not a common condition for someone so naturally even-tempered, but he found Annie's perfidy unforgiveable. All those stories she had told, about the apothecary being able to fly had spread from neighbour to neighbour and become accepted fact, and it was all her fault, the little tattle tale. And it was completely untrue. Jemmy pulled himself up abruptly. What was he thinking? Of *course,* it wasn't true. People do not transform themselves into birds and butterflies and flap off, do they? Jemmy's unaccustomed fury began to transfer itself to the supposedly sensible adults, who had taken the word of a nine-year-old and accepted it as truth. But most of all, his fury fell upon himself. How could he possibly have believed any of it, even for a moment? He was deeply ashamed. Had it been the sheer romance of becoming the apprentice of a man with magical powers? Not something you do every day. He had been swept away on a tide of intrigue and excitement, and now he was washed up on the shingle of reality like an old boot. No magic; in fact, no romance at all. Dr Thrift was just a man on the run. Jemmy's dreams collapsed round his ears and slumped in disappointment. It was a practical matter, nothing more.

'Shall we have a breath of air, Dr Thrift, while you tell me all about it?' Jemmy led the way outside, picking up the net and boathook he had left at the door. He could always think better when he was standing on shingle.

A Scurvy Knave?

Inspired by early scurvy-grass (*Cochlearia danica*), very common all along Chesil. Not actually a grass but packed with vitamin C and once used to prevent scurvy in sailors.

But who could possibly be pursuing the good and helpful Dr Thrift, apparently with evil intent? It was unthinkable.

'I promise you it's true,' said the apothecary, as they trudged along the ridge of the beach, just as if he'd read Jemmy's mind. 'I must get away.'

'But why ever would anyone be pursuing you, sir?'

Dr Thrift stopped, examining the pebbles. It was a guilty look, sure enough. 'Because I stole something of his.' There, it was out.

Of all things, Jemmy could not believe Dr Thrift was a thief. A thief, after all, needs presence of mind, and the apothecary spent much of his time holding rambling conversations with plants. No, he could never be a thief.

'What?' said Jemmy, disbelieving his own ears. 'Stole something? Stole what?'

'A large and beautiful gold coin,' said Dr Thrift, his eyes filling with tears. 'And I wish to the heavens I had never set eyes upon it.'

Not a small theft then, thought Jemmy in dismay.

'I stole it,' said Dr Thrift, extracting a linen herb-bag from his pocket and dabbing his eyes. 'I persuaded myself it was lost. Finders keepers, you know? But in my heart I knew this wasn't true. Of course, it belonged to someone. He must have counted the coins; there were many. He saw me looking and knew I had taken one.'

'It was only one coin,' said Jemmy, desperately seeking excuses.

'Indeed,' said the apothecary, 'but it had an owner, and he wants it back. Only to be expected.'

'But Dr Thrift, sir, can't you just give the coin back to him?'

'Bless your heart; no, Mr Herring. I spent it, you see? That was how I set myself up as an apothecary. Spent it all, to the last farthing. There is nothing to give back but my books, my bottles, my stock in trade. I should be ruined, and he would still not have his gold coin. *That* is what he wants: he has told me it is my last chance. He will return soon, and I must be gone before he does.'

The stranger in dark clothes. It all began to make sense. That man had not visited Dr Thrift as a friend; he had come to threaten him, to demand the return of the gold.

Jemmy chewed his lip, thinking.

'Then we must do something about it, sir,' he said.

The dilemma, as Jemmy saw it, was simple. Dr Thrift was guilty as charged, admitted it himself. He had not set out to steal anything, exactly, but he had picked up and kept something that did not belong to him. And the rightful owner was perfectly entitled to demand reparation, and punishment, too. Any court in the land, great or small, would agree to that. So, to assist the good doctor was to thwart the rule of law and would place Jemmy on the wrong side of it, too. This was not what he had anticipated when he had set out to become the apothecary's assistant.

Jemmy closed his mouth and drew himself up. 'Y' need not distress y' self, Dr Thrift,' he said earnestly. 'I will fight him. See 'im off for you.' He sincerely hoped the apothecary's pursuer might not be too good a fighter. 'I'll take care of you, sir.'

'Very kind,' said Dr Thrift, 'Oh, most thoughtful, but I fear you don't quite understand. My adversary is not an ordinary person: he is a most clever conjuror. Vindictive, you see. He has many powers. Can take on any form. I can only run away.'

Jemmy wished the apothecary would stick to shorter words. Vindictive, now what did that mean? He only understood that it was bad. However, he did have an idea what a conjuror was, and that was not to be believed. 'Oh, sir,' he said. 'You're pulling my leg, I believe.' The apothecary's expression showed otherwise.

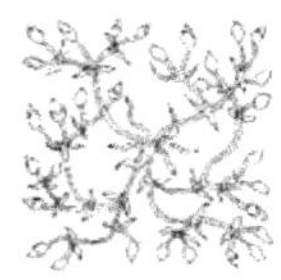

Stony-hearted

Inspired by rock samphire (*Crithmum maritimum*), an incredibly tough and tolerant seaside plant that grows directly on rock or shingle all along Chesil.

Jemmy stared at his bootlaces; the apothecary watching his face anxiously. What was a simple fisherman to think? Fighting a debtor was one thing, taking on a powerful conjuror was quite another. Not a fair fight at all. Dr Thrift had done a bad thing. He was a thief, and that was that. But he was not a bad man, not at heart. And Jemmy looked into his own heart and found it wanting: had he not decided to run away to avoid marrying Daisy, and all that it entailed? People would say that he had as good as jilted her. Not exactly a crime, but not Sunday-best behaviour, neither.

'We all have our failings, Mr Apothecary,' said Jemmy at last. 'It's not for me to judge you, whatever y' did. I'll help if I can.' *And if you will take me with you when you go.* It went unsaid, but both parties understood.

Dr Thrift let out a shuddering sigh of relief. 'That is very humane and kind, Mr Herring,' he said, 'but I don't know what's to be done, I'm sure.'

'We can defeat this conjuror,' Jemmy heard himself say. It was wild talk, and quite possibly dangerous, but Jemmy felt it was a change for the better. 'Tell me about him, please.' This sounded brave and bold in the face of feral magic.

'Well,' said Dr Thrift, 'to begin with, I know he is a thief himself, and an arsonist, to boot.'

Jemmy brightened; Dr Thrift may have done something wrong, but his pursuer had done worse.

The apothecary went on, 'He caused a terrible conflagration in the city, quite on purpose.'

'Conflag ... ' Again, Jemmy wished the apothecary would use shorter words.

'A fire, Mr Herring, very terrible. It blazed to the very sky. And while the people were thus diverted ... '

Diverted? thought Jemmy, *I should think they were!*

' ... he flew in and stole their gold. Piece by piece: from the guildhall, from the saddlers, the bakeries, the brewhouses.'

'When you say "flew" ... ' said Jemmy, puzzled.

'I mean flew, Mr Herring. This conjuror can turn himself into a magpie: a thieving magpie that found and took the gold, made a cache of it, and escaped the fire as the poor souls of the city could not.'

'And how do you know this, Dr Thrift?' Jemmy thought it a mighty tall story.

'Why, because he boasted of it, Mr Herring. Told me himself.'

'But what would make you believe such a thing?' asked Jemmy, still sceptical.

'Anyone would, Mr Herring,' said Dr Thrift, 'if
the conjuror turned himself into a magpie before their
eyes, perched on their shoulder, and chattered the story
into their very ears. And doubly distressing when you
had thought yourself responsible for that very fire.
"Written in my stars," they told me, and it wasn't me at
all. I found his cache of gold hidden in a tree-root, and
took one coin, just one. And he pursued me, Mr Herring,
in the forms of loathsome animals, delivering his
threats. I ran away, and I have run from him ever since.
What else could I do?'

'You, *we*, can stand up to this conjuror,' said
Jemmy, wondering if this were a very grave mistake. It
was only a very few moments before he found out.

Jemmy Makes a Stand

Inspired by sea aster (*Aster tripolium*), a plant once used as a treatment for the eyes, and perhaps just the thing to make everything clear!

The big black and white gull transformed itself before their eyes.

'It's the conjuror!' breathed Dr Thrift. 'Back already. I told you … oh, I said … '

The man before them smiled nastily. 'Well, apothecary, time is up. Give me back my gold or take the consequences.'

Jemmy forced himself forward and edged between the conjuror and the terrified apothecary.

'Well, well. And who is this bold knight? Come to save you, has he?'

Jemmy pulled himself upright, brandishing his net and boat hook and feeling seriously underprepared. The conjuror was not the wizened old man he had imagined, but no older than himself. Young and strong.

'Will you fight me, Jemmy Herring?'

How does he know my name? wondered Jemmy.

'Fight me as a black-back gull, will you? If I turn myself into one?'

Jemmy thought he could cope with that if he were careful of the beak.

'Fight me as an eagle, could you?'

Jemmy had never seen one, but he had a worrying notion of the size and potential armaments. His hand flew to the lucky shark's tooth on the bootlace round his neck. The conjuror followed the movement.

'Fight me as a great shark, would you, fisherman?' Jemmy was wondering whether this would be in the water or out and thinking that a boat hook was a tad underpowered as a weapon either way. But then his eye was caught by another black-back gull, veering out of a wave-trough, over the crest, and straight up the beach towards them, with a very determined look in its pale eye.

'I ... oooh,' said Jemmy, as the gull fastened its beak firmly on the conjuror's ear.

'Ow, gerroff!'

The gull let go and glided to the ground. 'I'm really most awfully sorry,' it said, before transforming itself into a tall grey-haired woman. 'But you know what children are like.'

Jemmy dropped his boat hook and almost speared his own foot.

The woman frowned and cuffed the conjuror round the ear. 'This is my son; I have been looking for him ever since that regrettable incident of the fire in the city and the stolen gold. *Most* embarrassing.' She cuffed him again.

'M-madam,' Dr Thrift had found his voice, 'you are his *mother*?'

Jemmy looked, open-mouthed, from the conjuror, to his grim-faced mother, to the clearly befuddled Dr Thrift.

'Stole my gold,' said the conjuror out of the corner of his mouth, pointing at Dr Thrift.

'It wasn't yours, y' little thief,' said his mother, cuffing him again. 'I had to pay it all back and bear the cost of the rebuilding. D' ye know how much it costs to restock an arsenal?' She rolled her eyes at Jemmy and Dr Thrift. 'And now I hear you turned yourself into a whale and sank a ship, forsooth.'

'I had to smoke him out, Mother, had to. I suspected he were here; knew he'd come out to sailors in distress.' The conjuror sneered. 'And out of the woodwork he came. And I had 'im, too, til you poked your nose in.'

His mother assumed an even more dangerous look. 'Never mind that. I have a ship-full of coals to pay for now. The cost is astronomical! Just wait until I get you home, you little brute.'

Dr Thrift recovered himself and stepped forward. 'I thank you very kindly, madam, for intervening, but the fact remains that I took a gold coin, whoever it might belong to. And I cannot pay it back.'

'Oh, I know that Mr Apothecary. I have already paid it back on your behalf. And given that you invested it in the good of others … I know how often you treat poor folks for no payment, let us say no more about it. I shall, however, have a lot more to say about it to *you*.' she added, turning to her son, who looked stricken.

And both of them turned back into black-back gulls, soaring off over the sea; the mother pecking tufts of feathers out of her son's tail. His mournful cries of 'Owk, owk, owk' echoed back to Jemmy and Dr Thrift as the birds faded into the distance.

'Well,' said Jemmy, 'I never expected *that.*'

Pebbles crunched as people, wary observers of the scene, scrambled up the beach behind him and Jemmy felt a small hand slip into his own.

'Annie?' he said, but it wasn't Annie. It was Daisy Goodship.

'Oh, Jemmy,' she breathed. 'You faced they magical creatures so bravely. They could'a turned you into a real herring, if they'd had a mind, but you stood your ground.'

Her face glowed with admiration, and Jemmy glowed too in the reflected light of her look; all his resolutions to escape crumbled to pieces. He squeezed her hand affectionately. Life with Daisy might not be such a bad thing after all.

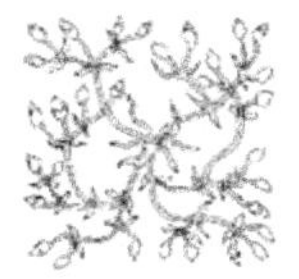

Chesil's Blessing

Inspired by Portland Spurge (*Euphorbia portlandica*), named for the isle at the very end of Chesil Beach, and so a fitting end for this story.

You would have thought the very pebbles of Chesil had eyes and ears, considering the speed with which the news of Dr Thrift's encounter with the conjuror spread along the beach. Once Jemmy had helped the apothecary back to his dishevelled black hut and made him comfortable, he had asked to be left in peace for a day or two. Jemmy had respected the request and chased off any curious sightseers who had wandered too close. On the third day, he and Annie, bearing bread, milk, and fresh fish, went to see how the apothecary was doing. They were surprised to find him outside and at work.

'Now then, Miss Annie,' Dr Thrift said, 'you can assist me, if you will, by running over to the meadow behind the beach – you know the place? Fetch me some of the best bitter buttercups; I think there are a few left. Just a couple of leaves, no more. We must be respectful of the plants, yes?'

'Oh, but Dr Thrift,' wailed Annie, 'there are nettles there. I do so hate them.'

The apothecary looked at her quizzically. 'Ah, yes. Hatred. I never quite got the hang of it myself. But is it not illogical, Miss Annie, to hate a plant for defending itself?'

'I am always stung,' cried Annie passionately. 'I hate them all!'

Dr Thrift assumed a grave expression. 'As a herbalist, I have seen many people consumed by hatred, beyond recall. No medicine can help when a person is being eaten up from the inside. It is the most destructive force I have encountered, and I heartily recommend that you do not indulge in it, Miss Annie, for your own sake.'

Annie looked mutinous. 'You *must* have hated the conjuror, though. He per … pers … '

'Persecuted me? He did. But I deserved it. I am still a sorry thief, whatever the excuses.'

Annie still looked doubtful.

'And besides,' said Dr Thrift, 'do you not know that the top-growth of the nettle makes a most nutritious soup? And that the stems can be woven into a very acceptable twine? Nothing is all bad, you know. Now cut along, and find me the leaves, if you please.'

Annie fled.

Jemmy, who had listened with interest, said, 'Surely, sir, you must have hated the people who called you "ill-starred"? They spoiled your future.'

'I did not,' said Dr Thrift. 'They thought it the truth, not said with malice, not really. The fact is, I should thank them all, the conjuror, too; they have made me who I am. And as you see, the future has not turned out so badly for me after all.'

'What will you do?' asked Jemmy, expecting an imminent departure.

'Oh,' said Dr Thrift, 'Well. I thought, if the local people agree, that I might stay here.'

Jemmy's face fell into visible confusion. He honestly didn't know whether this would be good or bad from his own viewpoint.

The apothecary looked at him keenly for a moment and then turned, saying over his shoulder, 'Of course, I should be very happy to have you and young Miss Annie as my apprentices. I have much to tell and teach, you know.'

Jemmy nodded, still in two minds.

Dr Thrift seemed to read his mind. 'Once you have the knowledge, Mr Herring, you may choose what to do with it, and where, and ... er, *with whom*. Even with Miss Goodship, should that idea suit you after all.' Jemmy blushed to the roots of his hat, and the apothecary smiled. 'Just as I suspected. And by the way, Mr Herring, there is no known cure for love: the potion I gave you will have improved your digestion, but nothing more.'

Jemmy gawped.

'Now, come along, do,' said Dr Thift. 'Miss Annie will be back with the leaves, and there is much to be done before winter sets in.'

The great beach of Chesil had nothing to say, but it rattled its pebbles in an agreeable way, as if to say, 'yes indeed, let it be so.'

The End

www.ingramcontent.com/pod-product-compliance
Lightning Source LLC
Chambersburg PA
CBHW070511170726
48291CB00008B/2704